THE CIRCLE OF LIFE SERIES - A

# Georgina Gets a New Mummy

Author: Brendah Gaine

Illustrator: Amy Brunskill

AuthorHouse™ UK
1663 Liberty Drive
Bloomington, IN 47403  USA
www.authorhouse.co.uk
UK TFN: 0800 0148641 (Toll Free inside the UK)
UK Local: 02036 956322 (+44 20 3695 6322 from outside the UK)

Because of the dynamic nature of the Internet, any web addresses or links contained in
this book may have changed since publication and may no longer be valid. The views
expressed in this work are solely those of the author and do not necessarily reflect the views
of the publisher, and the publisher hereby disclaims any responsibility for them.

Any people depicted in stock imagery provided by Getty Images are models,
and such images are being used for illustrative purposes only.
Certain stock imagery © Getty Images.

This book is printed on acid-free paper.

ISBN: 978-1-6655-8609-2 (sc)
ISBN: 978-1-6655-8610-8 (e)

Print information available on the last page.

Published by AuthorHouse 02/19/2021

# About the BOOK

This story deals with feelings of sadness and resentment as well as confusion.

Coping skills to address the feelings could be to join a group where you can listen to other children's stories and talk about your story. You can draw and talk about your drawings and play games.

# Acknowledgements

To my brother, Richard Parker, who is always willing to read my writing and provide useful insights and additional perspectives for me to consider, thank you for your encouragement and support of my passion for helping children find ways to cope with uncomfortable feelings.

To Rakesh Bhanot, a colleague, who wrote the Foreword.

To Amy Brunskill for the illustrations.

To David and Megan who have helped me with the intricacies of technological challenges.

# Foreword

There are numerous books, websites and YouTube videos on how to deal with grief (mourning, bereavement) that are available to parents, teachers, counsellors, therapists etc, but few, if any, approach this subject in the creative and sensitive way that Brendah Gaine has tackled it in this series of original short stories! They are not just tales for children to enjoy (sic.) as stories but also very effective heuristic vehicles for learning to deal with the trauma of grief. What is remarkable is that Brendah manages to create 10 completely different and poignant scenarios using so few words. Each protagonist 'feels' real; may be this is because they are all based on actual cases that Brendah dealt with in her professional work that spans over 40 years. The characters in the stories are real children that Brendah supported in South Africa. It is this depth of personal experience that enables her to 'translate' theories of grief (cf. Kubler-Ross et al) into practical strategies to enable children (even very young ones) to deal with the loss of a parent, a friend, or a sibling. Even without the additional helpful questions for discussion, and other suggestions for exploiting each story, the narratives themselves demonstrate how to cope with grief "in an appropriate way." The location of the 'case studies' may be South Africa but the suggested solutions in each story are appropriate for grieving children (and even adults) in any cultural setting. The themes addressed in the stories (anger, shyness, timidity, loneliness, building trust, parent-child relationships et al) are universal; as, indeed, are many of the practical ways of dealing the 'human' problems mentioned throughout the book, viz. slow breathing exercises, keeping a 'memory-box' of happy occasions relating to someone who has passed away, mindfulness, and even just accepting that "it's OK to sad," or "it's OK to cry."  This set of stories (each a separate publication) is not just a collection of moving 'slices of life,' together, they comprise a practical manual for parents, teachers and other professionals who work with children facing the loss of a loved one. I am sure, however, that all teachers who teach young children will find them useful and encourage their pupils to read them simply as good stories.

Rakesh Bhanot BA MA PGCE
Retired Principal Lecturer, Coventry University

# Dedication

*For David and Megan who have taught me to be sensitive to children's' feelings and to find ways to respond to the discomforts of loss and grief as we travel along life's journey together..*

# Introduction

These stories are written by Brendah Gaine who has practical experience in working with children who were traumatised by loss of family members and friends. For some it was sudden loss, while others saw loved ones suffer through illness. Regardless of circumstances, each child learn to cope with the trauma is a way that worked best for him or her. To help, we formed support groups in their schools for them to attend on a weekly basis at the end of the day. They all needed support to talk about their feelings, listen to the experiences of other children going through similar circumstances, and engage in activities that helped them to express their feelings emotionally and physically. They developed skills to cope with loss and learnt to grieve in appropriate ways.

Each story focusses on the feelings addressed and the coping skills. There are discussion questions so an adult can engage with the child about the issues addressed in the story. Advice is given about how the child can process the feelings brought up in the story. The books can be used by adults who are parents, therapists, nurses, health visitors, social workers, or teachers. Children may want to read them on their own.

When Georgina was seven years old, her mummy became very sick. For a short time, Georgina visited her in hospital every day. Everyone said her mummy would be home again soon. Even her mummy said so. But then suddenly the visits stopped.

"Is Mummy coming home today?" Georgina asked her dad.

"No, Georgina. Mummy won't be coming home again."

Georgina was confused. That didn't sound right. "What do you mean?"

Dad shook his head sadly and said, "Mummy died in hospital."

"Does that mean I won't see her ever again?"

"That's right," Dad said and sighed.

Georgina felt sad and lonely. All she could think of was Mummy saying, "I'll be home soon." Why hadn't Mummy kept her promise?

S he watched her older sister and brother closely to see if they were sad and lonely too. They didn't say much to her, but she noticed that they talked quietly to each other. Georgina felt left out. *What will happen to me now?* she wondered. *Maybe if I stay near Dad everything will be all right.*

But Dad was very busy. There were always people at the house talking to him about flowers for the funeral or putting a notice in the newspaper and on facebook. When Georgina asked questions about the funeral, her Dad told her, "Not now, Georgina. This is grown-up business." No one wanted to explain anything to her. She felt even sadder and lonelier than before.

Georgina stayed at home for a few days. But no one seemed to notice whether she was in the room or not. Most of the time, she would go and lie on her bed, bury her face in her pillow, and cry. She missed her mummy so much. She could always talk to her. Now no one wanted to talk to her.

After a while, Georgina's dad said she could go back to school. She was glad to see her friends again and listen to the teacher telling them new things. But days at school were quite short, and every day when she got home, there was no mummy to talk to. Dad was at work, and her brother and sister came home from school later than she did. So Georgina had to stay with their neighbour until her brother or sister collected her and walked her up the road to their own house. But still, there was no mummy to greet them.

Georgina noticed that Dad was coming home later and later. She felt as though she hardly saw him anymore. One morning before school she asked him, "Why do you come home so late?"

"I'm very busy at work," he said.

That night, Dad brought a lady home for supper. He told Georgina to call her Aunt Rosie. The next night, Aunt Rosie came for supper again. And the next. And the next. Georgina's sister and brother liked Aunt Rosie a lot, and Dad certainly liked her. But Georgina wasn't sure how she felt.

Aunt Rosie was rather bossy. She asked Georgina, "Have you washed your face?" and, "Have you brushed your teeth?" These were the kind of things Mummy used to ask, and it didn't seem right when Aunt Rosie asked them. But Aunt Rosie was spending more and more time at their house, especially over weekends. Soon it seemed as if she never went home! Then suddenly one morning Dad had some news.

"Aunt Rosie and I are getting married," he said. "Soon you will have a new mummy." Georgina couldn't believe it. *A new mummy?* she thought. *I don't want a new mummy.* But she didn't say anything because everyone seemed so happy. Georgina wasn't happy at all. In fact, she went to lie on her bed and cried and cried.

The only time Georgina felt better was when she was at school. Her teacher, Ms. Darling, was kind and gentle, and Georgina liked her very much. Ms. Darling always noticed when Georgina looked sad and when she looked bright. One day the class was discussing families, and Georgina began to feel unhappy.

"What is the matter, Georgina?" Ms. Darling asked.

"I'm going to have a new mummy," said Georgina glumly.

"And how do you feel about that?" Ms. Darling wanted to know.

"I don't know," said Georgina. "But I miss my real mummy very much."

"Your new mummy will learn to love you, too, Georgina. And you will always remember your real mummy."

When Dad and Aunt Rosie were married, Georgina's sister and brother started calling her 'Mummy'. But Georgina didn't. She didn't want to say, "Mummy," to someone who wasn't her mummy. Even when her daddy scolded her and told her to show respect, Georgina just couldn't do it.

Ms. Darling, her teacher, was worried about Georgina. She didn't want her to feel so sad. So at Parents' Evening, she spoke to Georgina's dad.

"I know she misses her mum", said Dad, "but I have a new wife now. And Georgina should be happy to have a new mother."

Ms. Darling thought about it for a while and then said, "Maybe it would help if Georgina had someone to talk to. There is a group of children that meets once a week after school. They have all been through a loss, and some of them now have new mothers and fathers. It might help if Georgina could hear their stories."

Dad agreed that it sounded like a good idea.

The first time Georgina went to the group, the children all played with clay and drew pictures of their families. They talked about how it felt when someone you love wasn't there anymore. After a while, Georgina told her own story. She explained how sad she felt and how much she missed her mummy. She told them about Aunt Rosie and how she was supposed to call her 'mummy'. Some of the other children also had new mothers. "It's not so bad," they said. "Our new mummies look after us just like our real mummies did."

Each week Georgina went back to the group. They sang songs and played games and talked some more. Whenever she came home, Aunt Rosie was waiting, and she always listened while Georgina told her about the day. Georgina showed her the pictures she had drawn, and Aunt Rosie said they were very good. Georgina didn't say so, but in her heart she thought, *I might be able to call her mummy one of these days.* Somehow it didn't seem so bad to have a new mummy after all.

# Questions to Work
# with Children

1. When Georgina was sad because her mummy had not kept her promise to come home from the hospital, Georgina felt that her mummy had not told her the truth. Has anyone told you something and then not kept his or her promise?

2. What can you do to feel better when someone does not keep a promise?

3. How do you think Georgina felt when her dad told them he was going to marry the lady he had brought to their home?

4. Do you think that Georgina liked going to the group?

5. How did the group help Georgina?

# processing your feelings

For dealing with the emotions experienced by the reader try reflecting on the feelings you are experiencing. Acknowledge them and connect with the feelings in your body. Become aware of the discomfort. Now clench your fists tight and breathe in. Hold your breath for a count of 3 and slowly breathe out to the count of 5. Do this 3 times. (You can do this with the child to help overcome the uncomfortable feelings.)

Now just stay still for a minute while you become aware of your surroundings and feel good about finding coping skills in a group.

Lightning Source UK Ltd.
Milton Keynes UK
UKHW050634280221
379520UK00002B/12